School of Fish

By Jane Yolen

Illustrated by Mike Moran

Ready-to-Read

Simon Spotlight
New York London Toronto Sydney New Delhi

SIMON SPOTLIGHT

An imprint of Simon & Schuster Children's Publishing Division

1230 Avenue of the Americas, New York, New York 10020

This Simon Spotlight edition July 2019

Text copyright © 2019 by Jane Yolen

Illustrations © 2019 by Mike Moran

For information about special discounts for bulk purchases, please contact
Simon & Schuster Special Sales at 1-866-506-1949 or business@simonandschuster.com.

Manufactured in the United States of America 0519 LAK

10 9 8 7 6 5 4 3 2 1

Library of Congress Cataloging-in-Publication Data

Names: Yolen, Jane, author. | Moran, Michael, 1957– illustrator.

Title: School of fish / by Jane Yolen ; illustrated by Mike Moran.

Description: New York : Simon Spotlight, [2019] | Series: School of fish |
Series: Ready-to-read. level 1 | Summary: A young fish confidently begins his first day of
school, but soon faces fear, anger, and other emotions by counting to ten, thinking of calm
seas, and making a new friend.

Identifiers: LCCN 2018047683 (print) | LCCN 2018052709 (eBook) |
ISBN 9781534438897 (hardback) | ISBN 9781534438880 (paperback) |
ISBN 9781534438903 (eBook)

Subjects: | CYAC: Stories in rhyme. | First day of school—Fiction. | Schools—Fiction. |
Fishes—Fiction. | BISAC: JUVENILE FICTION / Readers / Beginner. | JUVENILE
FICTION / Animals / Fishes. | JUVENILE FICTION / School & Education.

Classification: LCC PZ8.3.Y76 (eBook) | LCC PZ8.3.Y76 Sch 2019 (print) | DDC [E]—dc23

LC record available at https://lccn.loc.gov/2018047683

I'm sleek. I'm cool.

I'm off to school.

My pencils are stacked.

My lunch box is packed.

The water is nice.

I'm cool as ice.

Don't even have to
think it twice.

Where the path bends,

I'll meet new friends.

Fun while learning never ends.

I'm silver. I'm cool.

I'm off to school.

But what's ahead?

It's cold. It's dark.

I see the head

of a great big shark.

I need to swim fast,
race and hide.

The shark's big mouth
seems awfully wide.

TEETH! TEETH!
TEETH! TEETH!

There are hundreds above
and hundreds beneath.

I dodge and tangle
in the weeds.
I do not have
what a school fish needs.

But then I see
that on its side,
there is a door
that opens wide.

BUS! BUS! BUS!

It is safe

to go inside.

There are so many fish
but just one me.
I'm as alone
as I can be.

Wait! Count to ten.
Think about calm seas,
and then . . .

I'm slick. I'm cool.

I enter school.

I really miss
my mom and dad.

And then some fingerling
makes me mad.

I bump into
an electric eel.

Or maybe it's a whale
or seal.

Wait! Count to ten.
Think about calm seas,
and then . . .

I look around.

What do I see?
Here is another
fish like me.

A little scared.

A little new.

All alone

and feeling blue.

I show her how
to count to ten,
think about calm seas,
and then . . .

Whew!
I'm really ready
to be in school.

We're steady. We're ready.
And we're *real* cool.